THE CORPORATE EXISTENCE

My corporate sage wasn't without its fair share of surprises, it did not seem right from the beginning and I found myself in a mess as always. With shades of love capturing my attention, my mind was engrossed in the subtleties of the human faculty of love, besides the betrayals of the bad corporate existence.

many months back. I found myself in a new city and began staying in a hotel room. The office wasn't what I had imagined it to be. My mind had pictured a big glass building with a dozen floors and a big lounge which led to an entrance filled with cubicles and cabins.

But unlike the image, it was a small two floored residential converted into an office. The entrance was narrow and there was no crowd of candidates waiting for the interview on that fateful day.

It was past noon as I quickly hurried inside the office building. I was greeted by an old lady at the desk.

spoke.

"I am here for the walk in interview. I was referred by a friend who had seen the job ad," I mentioned.

"Ok, give me your resume and please take a seat," she said.

I could hear the loud discussion happening inside the room,

finishing the interview while I waited, I thought.

The next candidate went inside and I started reading the magazines kept there. I was trying to take my mind away from the interview anxiety.

"Excuse me!" Spoke a female voice. As I looked up, I found a traditionally dressed lady looking attractive face and appeared well groomed. She had a file in her hand.

“Can you move slightly?” she questioned. It appeared as if she wanted to sit down beside me. The office entrance was cramped with just a single sofa for the visitors. It felt as if she was in a hurry to sit down after rushing inside the office. I could panting she was subjecting herself to.

I moved and gave space for her to sit. She got up and gave her resume to the old lady at the desk. So, she was here for the interview too, I thought. The smell of her perfume lingered and aroused my senses to no end.

was conducted in an informal setting. The two people in the panel were cracking jokes and asking me about my hobbies. It was nothing like what I had expected. They did pose some serious job related questions in between though.

I left after the interview, as I watched the stranger lady go inside for her interview turn. I bad of me, I thought. I was informed that the selected will be intimated over a phone call in a few days time.

I had few days to waste, so decided to sleep it out and kill my time using daydreaming as my tool.

A few days had passed, it was nearing noon when my pleasant

ringing sound of my phone. It was the good news I was eagerly expecting. I was selected for the job.

I couldn't stay for long in the hotel I was put up in. It was almost a week since I arrived and the money I carried was running out. I was supposed to join the new office starting Monday the coming week. With just few days for me to do was to continue staying in the hotel room until my job starts.

I got dressed and left for my new office with high expectations and a tinge of anxiety. I wondered if the beautiful lady would show up and whether she was selected. Her thoughts consumed my mind.

desk this time around, and I was instead greeted by a young stylish guy who had spiked hair and studs. He greeted my presence with a prolonged good morning.

"Hi! I am Rizwan!" He spoke, and offered a handshake, which I promptly acknowledged.

admin team member as he guided me to my desk. There were three other empty cubicles in that room.

"You will receive the induction email shortly. The team lead will meet you and guide you on the project. There is one more new joiner who has already joined today," he mentioned.

wondered who the other new joiner was. I kept hoping that it would be the same lady I had seen on the interview day.

My doubts were laid to rest shortly as I heard her voice calling out to me from behind. Yes, it was indeed her and she looked pretty in that bright yellow churidar she wore. It seemed to be such a perfect fit, for her.

"Can you come to the training room? I think you must have got that email too," she inquired.

I hadn't checked and in fact the first thing I did on the office computer was to login to Facebook and update my new job status. It read "Started a New Job."

I got up mesmerised and followed her into the training room which was on the first floor. I was besotted by her presence. The perfume lingered in the air as I followed the trail and went upstairs behind her.

The training room wasn't full but had two people who seemed eager for our presence. We went a loud hello.

"Please sit down. Welcome to our team. I am Mahesh, the team lead for the project," a fat man with a big belly spoke from his seat. It was evident that he would have a hard time in getting up and sitting down at short intervals. The other person in the room was Rizwan.

introduction? You both can introduce each other," the man continued.

Before I could get up and start with my intro talk, she held onto my hand as if to suggest that she wanted to go first. I held back and let her get up to talk.

"Hello everyone, I am Kalpana and I have done my masters in

for a college as a lecturer. I have three years of experience in teaching. I am very much looking forward to this opportunity and hope to learn new things," she spoke confidently.

I got up next and quickly wrapped up my intro. Mahesh did not seem amused, he might have been expecting more from me, I thought. After highlighting us both that he will be training us individually, as this was a new project for the firm and the project had custom requirements.

The project involved marketing functions for a new food joint which was looking to spread its operations throughout the city. The food joint was less than a year old and was looking for innovative marketing campaigns.

Kalpana was seated in a different room to mine. I wasn't entirely convinced with this idea as I felt we should sit next to each other especially being on the same project. Maybe, Rizwan was behind this arrangement, or it was that fat guy Mahesh, I thought. After all, Kalpana was the other room.

The other three cubicles in my room were occupied by Rizwan and the remaining admin staff. The three boys used to keep talking in between and would overlook my desktop once in a while, as if to make sure that I was working, or at least pretending to be working, by terms.

The first lunch break arrived on the first day, and the training hadn't begun so far. Rizwan told me that there was a place to eat at the rooftop with chairs and tables placed. The employees would assemble there and eat. It was also used for informal gatherings or occasions apparently.

I did not find Kalpana as I passed the other room, her desk was empty and Mahesh wasn't there too. I took the stairs to the roof. The building was a residential one and the second floor was occupied on rent by a family.

On reaching the roof, my eyes searched for that lady in yellow. She was there and munching on something, sitting next to glance and smiled at me. I reciprocated.

I sat next to Rizwan who offered me a piece from his bread sandwich. He dipped the bread in that native mutton curry he had got. Being a vegetarian, I only took few bites from the sandwich without the dips to please him. I did not feel hungry surprisingly.

direction and my eyes met hers, she was looking at me too and it felt as if she wasn't enjoying the conversation with Mahesh, who appeared to be nagging her.

Rizwan left, and I was sitting alone for a while. I was thinking about few past events and looking up at the afternoon sky. "Can I sit here?" My thoughts question.

“Yes! Sure!” I replied.

“So, you are new to the city?” She asked. She must have heard my intro talk in which I had made a passing reference to my previous job in another city, I thought.

now," I replied.

"How is your first day going? Did Mahesh start training you?" I continued.

"Not yet. He was sharing about himself and his family. He is struggling with getting his kid admitted to a new school apparently," she said.

fashion. I was eager to know more about Kalpana and her life. Mahesh and his story did not fancy my interest one single bit.

The thing I found pleasing was the fact that Kalpana seemed to be equally interested in knowing about me or so I thought. She was smiling in between and maintaining that eye contact for longer than expected with a stranger to her, I thought.

We kept looking at each other for a while before I realized that it was just the two of us sitting there now. Mahesh had left in between and apparently I had even failed to notice this. Our attention seemed to be just on each other.

it was already past the lunch break time. “We must be going down Kalpana. I think the lunch break is over,” I spoke.

“Gosh! Yes, come soon,” she exclaimed, after getting up quickly. She rushed towards the stairs in a hurry. I followed her, after quickly washing my hands in the tap on the roof.

got back to her desk. I saw Mahesh starting to talk to her immediately.

The first day passed uneventfully and I left to the hotel room. She wasn't in the room while I left office, so I thought that she might have left by then.

I wanted to shift from the hotel room and was looking for a

informed a broker through a friendly hotel staff. The broker wanted me to meet him in the evening to see a house and decide. He had claimed over the call that it was an independent two bedroom house with each room housing two beds. One bed had got free as someone had vacated recently.

just meeting my expectations. It wasn't exactly an occupant friendly accommodation with a sewage canal nearby and a slum. The place was the breeding ground of aggressive mosquitoes that were blood thirsty. But the mesh was helping, and once inside, the house seemed to do the job pretty well. I decided to move there at the earliest and in the new city had indeed started.

My shifting was done and the office days started passing quickly too. Before long, almost a month had passed. The same routine ensued everyday with me, and the weekends were spent sleeping.

The training program was completed and the project

like, so far so good, as we hadn’t heard any critical comments from the client.

Kalpana had begun spending more time with me, and there was increased fondness amongst us. I shared my childhood stories too with her, and she listened to them with rapt attention.

resigned to our closeness and his interruptions had considerably reduced, Rizwan, on the other hand, kept a keen eye on us while we spoke and he did crack the occasional joke.

One day as we sat for lunch, Kalpana did not seem like her usual self. There was something different, and we ate quietly as she shared her food with me.

“I am not hungry today. Can you finish my lunch box too?” She asked me.

“Ok! Not a problem,” I said, loved her home cooked food.

“Are you ok? You are behaving so differently today. Is everything ok?” I questioned her politely.

to tell you but haven't told you yet," she spoke.

"Go on, I am all ears. What is it?" I replied.

She continued, "I am going through a personal crisis and it has been tough for me. I do not know how to say this to you but I feel I should, sooner rather than later."

I nodded to suggest that she continue talking and had got really curious by now, eager to know what she was about to reveal.

"Many here don't know about this and I haven't told you too. I got married a year back, before I moved here," she spoke, with a straight face.

puzzled and confused. All this while, I was under the impression that she was unmarried, there was nothing about her which suggested that she was already married. There was no vermillion, nor any trace of the married lady demeanour in her.

I was speechless, as she continued talking.

nuances of her troubled marriage with George, her so called husband, how they had fallen in love and how she had fought with her family to get married to him, and finally on how they had successfully eloped and got married.

I was still speechless and kept looking at her with my confused look. Finally, I spoke, “Why are that too now?"

On hearing this, she had tears swell up. I was taken aback and quickly got up from my chair, hadn't got the slightest idea on how to deal with the situation, my mind wasn't working.

The others at the rooftop place had left by now. I reached out to her as if to comfort her, and tried could realize what was happening, she had got up and hugged me tightly. This did not seem like a friendly hug to me and nor was it a consoling hug which she consented to. This seemed more like the way too passionate lovers hug each other while they got intimate. I was perplexed.

spoke, slowly relaxed her grip around me and making her sit on the chair. She had a handkerchief in her hand, which I used to wipe her swelling tears. “Please relax,” I appealed again.

She spoke after a while, “I truly loved George but things aren’t the way I had imagined it to be, we have bad fights and yesterday

My life feels miserable now."

After getting back to my desk, my mind was confused about the whole situation. It was not as much about what she had shared, but more about her overt expression of affection towards me.

That night back in my room, my mind was so full of Kalpana. Her

But, the fact that she was married and her story shook me up.

One fine day I realized that I was in love with Kalpana or so I thought. But something held me back from making it apparent.

The revelation had come to me the day I found out she was unhappily married. The through after I had finally managed to pop the question at the most inappropriate time.

"Are you serious Kalpana?" I questioned.

She replied, "I have started liking you and it's true. Yes, I love you, but I am confined to my marriage and hence helpless."

encourage her or to thwart her away, she did seem serious but somewhere I felt confused, especially considering her recent behaviour.

I just kept quiet and watched her as she looked at me and stroked her hair again. Her grip on my fingers had tightened. She felt ready to make an overt advance emotion.

Nevertheless, she got up and pulled me up too, we hugged it out, but I was doing it half-heartedly. She was weeping and saying that she wasn't happy with George, I did not react.

We got back to work and the days began to pass as usual. Her "miss you" texts on the instant considering she sat in the next room.

She told me all about her favourite movies and songs through the texts and kept insisting that I sing for her. Somewhere I felt drawn to her like never before. I had almost begun to feel like a saviour to her, someone ordained to free ordeal.

While all this was playing out and the so called affair was being discussed and dissected every other day, a foreigner entered our office and this happened exactly on Kalpana's birthday.

As was the norm, the cake cutting ceremony was supposed to happen before the lunch attendance too, he was introduced in the morning as an outside consultant representing a new client, and who was here purely on a business requirement.

The birthday celebration also saw me singing for Kalpana as I was compelled by the others in the office, the ethical me was as after all she was married.

My soulful rendering of the song was met with a big round of applause. After I had finished, Kalpana immediately walked towards me in front of all the other staff in the office and gave me a tight hug. All the others were speechless too just like me. I had expected a handshake and in front of everyone.

Before the interactions with the foreigner grew, it happened on one uneventful week day, the news from Rizwan in office was that George had found out about our alleged affair and Kalpana was stressed.

"You need to back out man. Don't ruin their marriage,"

there was news that she was expecting and would be on a pregnancy leave. I was taken aback but decided to let it pass and maintain my composure.

But the thoughts of Kalpana troubled me more than ever before. I spent sleepless nights thinking about her. The fact that she was pregnant had shaken me. All her claims of harassment meaningless now.

One night I was woken up by the loud ringing of the phone.

"Hello!" I answered.

After a long pause, I was greeted by a drunken voice of a man.

"I am George! Kalpana's husband," the voice claimed. He

from being unstable.

"Yes! Tell me? What is it?" I answered, after composing myself.

"Stop! Stop! Stop! Chasing my wife and disturbing her. She is fed up of you and does not want you to talk to her anymore. Do you hear me?" He sounded irritated.

Before I could respond, I heard Kalpana’s voice through the phone, but this time there was no sweetness in it.

She spoke, “Hello! Listen! Stop interfering in our life and disturbing me, stay away from me. Get out of my life and do not talk to me from now. I want to tell you that “I HATE YOU.” Bye!”

Kalpana's phone number. I wanted to be done with her for good, or at least I was willing to try and erase her memories.

The next day I decided to focus on bigger and better things and get acquainted with the foreigner who had joined few days back. Our conversations had started and we were getting to know each other.

Nick was indeed different and stood out from the rest. In few days, Kalpana had departed too on her pregnancy leave, saving me from crossing paths with her again.

Nick got along well with me, and we were put into the same training program, we were supposed to work on a new project together. Nick who was assigned a lead role in the project.

Nick was shrewd and smart. After flying in straight from Paris, he was nothing like the typical project lead Mahesh. Eccentric and raw in his ways, he felt like an alien, but I found myself identifying with him. The training process was going on smoothly with Nick always insisting that I waiting for anyone, as I found out.

Few weeks had passed and one night I found myself dreaming of Kalpana. We were fighting with each other to get married, the dream ended abruptly with a loud thud. I had accidently knocked off the Bluetooth speaker kept at the edge of the bed. It had landed on the water hence causing the thud.

I found myself in contemplation about the weird dream, and I wondered what she was up to. The weekend had started and I couldn't stop myself from wanting to verify the veracity of Kalpana's claim about her troubled marriage. More than anything, I felt that this was needed for my own mental kind of a closure.

I knew it was futile, but nonetheless felt the chase was needed. I needed to know things for my own satisfaction. I wasn't able to let go, even though I had wished her well and forgiven her.

Rizwan had once told me that Kalpana lived in a rented home

place and decided to explore.

"What are you doing this weekend?" I inquired, over the phone with Rizwan.

"Nothing much man, planning to catch up on a new movie with my current girlfriend," he answered.

but he never did mention about it, I thought.

"I want to meet you bro," I told him. I dared not mention about Kalpana and my intentions to track her, especially since he knew the whole history of things. I wondered if Kalpana had lied to him and painted me as a bad villain who tried to play the marriage breaker.

I had seen George's photo on social media after my primary research. I had researched after the threat call as I wanted to understand the speaker better. I had a vague or a fabricated idea of a villainous husband, thanks to the constant rant by Kalpana, claiming abuse and intimidation. All those might have been blatant lies and I wanted to verify the truth, but I could vouch for the that call.

Rizwan and me, we set out on his abused bike. I had devised a plan mentally as we started, and did not want us to go too far and leave the area. I tugged at his shirt suggesting we stop near the bakery around the corner, and munch on a few snacks. It was almost noon and not the ideal snack time but he stopped hot tea and a sandwich, before beginning our conversation over food.

I did not want to mention Kalpana directly, so indirectly asked him about the area. Knowing that he was the proverbial loudspeaker meant that he would spill the beans out on the information I needed, conversation.

"Do you know anyone else from our office that lives in this area? What about Mahesh?" I questioned, acting unaware and innocent the whole time. I had posed this question out of the blue, in between our conversation. We were discussing new car models with each other and this question

Without realizing things, he spilled the whole information out.

"Yes Bro! Kalpana stays in a house on that road. She and her husband stay on the ground floor of the third house on the right side," mentioned Rizwan, pointing towards the road next to the bakery. I was surprised that we had stopped exactly at the thought.

While we ate, Rizwan suddenly pulled my hand and pointed at something. I could see a car passing by but nothing that would captivate my attention. It looked like a brand new car, and maybe he was showing me the car, I thought.

with attention this time and it was none other than Kalpana, sitting on the back seat with a man who appeared familiar. It was George. My god, I had spotted her, what a double coincidence, I thought.

I could clearly see that she was resting her head on George's shoulder and who in turn appeared to be stroking her hair

Public display of affection, I thought, wasn't amused though.

"There they go," spoke Rizwan, as he giggled and continued, "They have purchased a new car I guess, and maybe going out for a drive. I hardly see her these days, today is an exception. Maybe, since you are here this happened," he laughed.

under the impression that she was single when she joined the firm, until I heard about her marriage. Although she stayed so close by, I had never spotted both of them together back then."

I quickly diverted him from the topic and decided to abandon the futile chase, the truth was as clear as daylight to me. She was we were together. I decided to rest my case and move on with my current uninspiring life. Firstly, get through the promotion cycle and then take things forward from there, I was thinking.

We rode along and before long the rather short feeling weekend had ended. I was back to my new desk. I was shifted to the first to the training room. I had Nick for company and had become more punctual, ever since we had started working together.

Nick and me, we were spending more time with each other than ever before and spoke on everything in addition to the usual work plans. We used to spend the lunch session discussing spirituality and

That was our common point of interest. Nick told me about the business world and its quirkiness.

He spoke about hostile takeovers, conflict of interest, intellectual property violations, insider information, and whistleblowers. Although I was aware of all these, I found his insights and information rather anyone would find in the book.

I wondered why someone like Nick, who was here just to train the employees on the new project and leave, talk about things like these, but I kept my suspicious and sceptical mind at bay.

I never wished that my suspicions would come to pass,

that I was a loyal employee of the company. I wasn't prepared for something like that.

"What are you doing Nick?" I inquired, as I came in one morning. I saw Nick accessing something on the computer assigned to me.

"Hey! Hi! It's nothing. I came in and saw your system running, replied.

I wondered if I had not logged out the prior day, if my memory served me well, then I felt I did, and had shut the system down too. I kept these doubts to myself without confronting Nick.

Nick got back to his laptop and started working furiously on it. He was updating data and I saw files on a private cloud. I had seen him do that on occasions but never questioned him, as after all, he was just here to train me and the new team which had to be formed. Also considering our offline rapport, it was increasingly difficult for me to question him or cast aspersions on his role and work.

me and gave me a hug before leaving for the day, this had never happened since the time he was here, but I chose to ignore the 'why now' question. He also shook my hands as he left. That was to be the last time I ever saw him, as I found out the next day.

A cloudy and gloomy day unfolded into an eerie day at the

heard people whisper. I heard people talking in the training room as I switched on my computer. Nick wasn't there. Rizwan rushed from the training room on hearing the sound of my presence.

"Come in quick. No need to start the system now," he spoke, holding my hand and pulling me towards the training room. As I the other members in the management. All of them appeared to be in a pensive mood and seemed to be eagerly waiting for me.

I entered and took a seat, Rizwan sat next to me. We all looked at each other and I was confused as to what had transpired.

from our company server?" The Director questioned me.

I did not know what to say, "No! I don't think so," I replied.

The Director continued, "There is a bad news that I am about to share with you. Today morning we found our server compromised, it was missing a large chunk of survey data. We it was Nick. His phone is also switched off and we found out that he has checked out yesterday night from the hotel where we were hosting him."

"He has escaped with all the data we believe. The data was from surveys we conducted on various client company products in the Indian market, and we wonder why he would do

Director.

The Director further explained, “We had an early morning call with the client regarding this but apparently they have no idea. Nick was indeed on their pay roll and he was sent on their behalf to train the team here. He used to give them regular updates, but they haven’t heard from him since the past few days. His back and he had stopped the updates shortly after that."

The expression of worry on the Director's face was palpable, and he continued to explain the situation. He said, "The client waited for the weekly update tomorrow but were taken aback when we disclosed things to them today. They have washed their hands off Nick and we the contract they have signed with us. It absolves them of a rogue trainer and only has terms of non-disclosure after the project team has been set up and approved."

I wasn't surprised, my suspicions were vindicated. I sat there thinking about my past interactions with Nick, while looking at the worried Director.

employees of the company were apprised of the situation early morning through email, which probably explained the eerie silence I encountered while I walked in on the day.

Nick was a SPY!

www.ingramcontent.com/pod-product-compliance
Lightning Source LLC
LaVergne TN
LVHW041129150826
845673LV00007B/2250

* 9 7 9 8 8 4 6 2 6 4 9 8 4 *